THE NEANDERTHALS ARE BACK

A Series of Stories about Modern Day Neanderthals and their New Families After Two Scientists Bring Them Back

THE BEGINNING

by Gini Graham Scott, Ph.D.

THE NEANDERTHALS ARE BACK

TABLE OF CONTENTS

INTRODUCTION 5
WHY BRING BACK THE NEANDERTHALS? 7
  How We Can Bring Back the Neanderthal 7
  What Happens If We Bring Back the Neanderthals? 9
  Introducing the Neanderthal Stories 12
THE BEGINNING 13
CHAPTER 1: DISCOVERY 15
  Morning 16
  The Experiment 18
CHAPTER 2: LEARNING IN THE LAB 21
CHAPTER 3: LEAVING THE LAB 25
CHAPTER 4: THE GROUP HOME 31
CHAPTER 5: GETTING TO KNOW THE KIDS 35
CHAPTER 6: A DAY TO REMEMBER 41
CHAPTER 7: THE AFTERMATH 51
CHAPTER 8: WHAT'S NEXT? 57
MORE ON THE SERIES 65
THE NEXT STORIES IN THE SERIES 67
  2: Get Smart 67
  3: The New Child 67
  4: The Boxing Match 67
  5: The Accusation 67
  6: The Competition 67
  7: Neanderthal Games 67
  8: The Robbery 67
  9: Rape! 67
  10: Sex Games 67
  11: Strike! 67
  12: Keeping Up with the Neanderthals 67
  13: Between Two Worlds 67
ABOUT THE AUTHOR 69

INTRODUCTION

WHY BRING BACK THE NEANDERTHALS?

I've been thinking about Neanderthals for the last three years and have been fascinated to read about the latest scientific discoveries about them. Among some of the discoveries that got me thinking are these:

- The Neanderthals spread out in Northern Europe, where they lived in small family groups, much like our early Hominoid ancestors.

- At some point, perhaps 100,000 to 30,000 years ago, early humans and Neanderthals interbred before the humans wiped them out. Now many of us with northern European and Asian roots have about 2% of Neanderthal DNA, which could include me.

- The Neanderthals had fire and burned it in fire pits. They obtained it from natural events like lightning strikes and forest fires and then tended the fire to keep it going. They also could make it by smashing mineral pyrite against flint to create sparks they nursed into a large fire.

- The Neanderthals made jewelry, cared for their sick, and buried their dead in common burial sites.

- They had language and the skills to communicate in order to organize small groups to hunt down game -- a skill which animals such as wolves use while hunting in packs to trap and kill their prey.

Taking all of that information together, I imagined that the Neanderthals might have had the brain power of a modern four, five, or six year old. Then, I wondered about the possibility of bringing the Neanderthals back, since there have been some recent developments in bringing back once extinct species.

How We Can Bring Back the Neanderthal

As I researched the matter, I discovered that scientists are talking about the science and ethics of bringing back

Neanderthals, now that they have some new techniques to bring back some mammals from extinction. One is the Pyrenean Ibex, the first mammal brought back briefly and there are continuing efforts to bring it back by cloning it from preserved cells, according to an article "Fresh Effort to Clone Extinct Animal" by Paul Rincon in the BBC news. Likewise, Australian scientists are working on bringing back the extinct Tasmanian tiger using a technique developed by Harvard geneticist George Church, according to several news articles, including one by Peter Devlin for the *Daily Mail* in Australia: "'It's Not Science Fiction, It's Science Fact': Australian Scientists Plan to Clone the Tasmanian Tiger and Bring It Back from Extinction and by John Pickrell explaining the process for Cosmos Magazine: "Return of the Living Thylacine." And under the leadership of George Church there is an effort to clone the mammoth using the DNA of closest living relative, the Asian elephant. In fact, a California Institute called Revive and Restore is where Ben Novak and other "de-extinction" engineers hope to use genetic engineering to revive selected extinct animals using the CRISPR gene editing tool.

In other research developments, scientists are now growing Neanderthal/human hybrid brains in a lab. Professor Svante Paabo, an evolutionary geneticist at the Max Planck Institute for Evolutionary Anthropology and author of *Neanderthal Man: In Search of Lost Genomes,* has already led an international team of scientists to successfully unravel the Neanderthal genome. To this end, the team has been using CRISPER gene-editing techniques to study the development of brains to determine what makes us human.

Thus, bringing back the Neanderthal is scientifically possible. George Church, the Harvard geneticist, believes cloning a Neanderthal in our lifetime is possible, using current stem cell technology and a completed sequence of the Neanderthal genome. It involves inserting a cell with the DNA obtained from Neanderthal bones and nurturing it in the body of a human female or a lab environment. Then, nine months later, a Neanderthal baby!

This approach is even closer to reality now through the Neanderthal Genome Project, a collaboration between several U.S. companies, scientists, and Germany's Max Planck Institute. As described in a *Science* article, "Can We Bring Neanderthals Back" by Robert Lamb, the process involves extracting DNA from bones, removing any contaminant DNA from bacteria or humans, and reconstructing the genome from decayed and chemically altered fragments. The artificial DNA then needs to be packaged into a cell, a process now being developed. Alternatively, if the DNA is put into a stem cell, it can be cultured and implanted into a human or blastocyst, a structure that exists very early when the embryo is first developed. The resulting embryo is a mix of mostly Neanderthal and some human features.

Though scientists have not yet produced a Neanderthal baby, the research shows it is possible, while current research has focused on finding drugs or other treatments to help humans. For instance, scientists have been studying the effects of Neanderthal genes in human tissues, and they have already created mice with Neanderthal genes. Soon they will have Neanderthal cell lines, tissues, and organs.

What Happens If We Bring Back the Neanderthals?

Given that a Neanderthal baby is in the realm of possibility, scientists have started debating the ethics of doing so. One example is the controversy swirling around a scientist in China, He Jiankui, who edited the human genome to produce twin girls. Once his work became known, this provoked a scandal, because he flouted the current norms for safety and human protections. As a result, he was censured by the Guandong health ministry where he worked and was fired from his university for inadequate safety testing and not following standard procedures. Inappropriately, he offered to cover the costs of fertility treatments and related expenses and required participants to repay the costs if they dropped out, which could be considered coercive. An additional concern was that he could have inadvertently caused mutations in other parts of the genome, causing unpredictable health consequences, though Jiankui claimed he found no such mutations. Meanwhile, a third gene-edited baby is on the way. Some other scientists were aware of his work but said nothing until after Jiankui announced the birth of the twin girls with edited genomes. After that, the scandal erupted and gained international attention.

He Jiankui's story shows that the idea of producing a Neanderthal baby is highly controversial. Yet it is still likely to happen, like most new breakthroughs in science, because a few courageous scientists are likely to work with the new technologies before they are accepted. In fact, their breakthrough is what will lead to the debate and ultimate acceptance, if their scientific efforts are successful.

In the case of the Neanderthals, some of the questions raised are:

- Will they be able to eat a regular human diet, since they might not have the necessary mutations to digest dairy products and processed grains?
- Will they be susceptible to common diseases or pathogens to which humans are immune?
- Will they enjoy a decent quality of life?
- What if the Neanderthal is naturally aggressive? How can that be controlled? Will drugging or confinement be necessary?
- Should a Neanderthal child be placed in captivity like some kind of zoo animal?
- Will the child face a lifetime of study?
- What developmental issues will an imperfectly genetically re-engineered Neanderthal experience due to birth defects?

- Can the Neanderthals pose a threat to modern humans - - though scientists consider this unlikely, or can we keep them alive and safe from us, which scientist consider the biggest threat?
- What kind of habit will be most suitable for these de-extincted Neanderthals, since our species has taken over the once prime habitats where they used to live?
- Since humans played a major role in the original extinction of Neanderthals by competing with them for food and homes and maybe giving them lethal diseases, will we recreate history and cause them to become extinct again?
- What will happen if humans interbreed with the new Neanderthals to create half-human, half-Neanderthal babies?
- Once Neanderthals are raised outside of scientific labs and facilities, where will they live? Will they live in group homes? With adoptive families?
- Will Neanderthals be given the rights of ordinary humans or be treated more like animals or pets?
- How will Neanderthals be educated to adapt to a modern society?
- How will modern humans react to Neanderthals in the community?
- What kind of jobs can Neanderthal's do, assuming their lower intelligence and aggressive nature?
- What will happen if a Neanderthal commits a crime, though they may not understand our ideas about crimes?
- What will happen if Neanderthals become victims?
- Will Neanderthals become a new underclass of society, who may easily become poor underpaid workers or even slaves,

Introducing the Neanderthal Stories

In sum, there are many issues that will occur if Neanderthal's are brought back to modern society. I have written this book of fictional stories after thinking about these different issues. They are based on the premise that scientists can bring back the Neanderthals, initially raise them in special facilities, and thereafter find them a place to live in a local community, where they face these various issues and more.

More specifically, *The Neanderthals Are Back* is a series of interconnected stories based on the initial premise that a paleontologist brings back some DNA from a Neanderthal burial ground discovered in an archeological dig in Northern Europe. He then works with a scientist friend to bring back some Neanderthal babies using stem cell, cloning, and CRISPER techniques, along with the help of some surrogate mothers. Then, these Neanderthal babies are raised in secret for their first few years of life in a laboratory setting, where they learn some simple language skills and tasks, such as farm labor, gardening, and routine factory assembly.

These stories look at what happens to the Neanderthals and those who live with them, care for them, employ them, or interact with them under varying social circumstances, such as in in school, at work, and in public events.

For now, I have written 13 short stories. But I see this as the beginning of an expanded series -- as books, as a TV or cable series, or a film developed from one or more of these stories.

So now, I invite you to meet the Neanderthals and experience their stories.

THE BEGINNING

CHAPTER 1: DISCOVERY

It was another snowy day in northern Norway. Darryl Jonas pulled the canvas doors of his tent back, hoping the storm would break soon, so the team of paleontologists he headed could return to the field and continue digging. They had already found some fossilized logs and ash, suggesting an ancient campfire of the Neanderthals. He was hopeful the crew could find some burial artefacts, even some remains of bones, once they could start digging again.

Darryl lit his lamp with a match and sat back on his sleeping bag. As he often did in these quiet alone moments, he pulled out his small binder with photos of his wife Annie and two kids, 4-year old Sammy and 6 year-old Jimmy. Just gazing at them made him feel better, like a reminder of why he continued to do this difficult work, because he had the support of his family, as well as his dedication to science and desire to do something more to stand out and be honored in his field.

"Yes, I know you're all still here for me," he thought as he moved the photo up and down between his hands, like the movement was making the image seem even more present and alive.

He thought about their last day, before he flew to Norway. They had gone to the county fair for an exciting fun-filled day, so they would have that lasting memory of him while he was gone for six weeks. Also, he wanted to enjoy an exhilarating last day with his wife, so there would be no time for regrets and talks about how much they would each miss each other while he was gone. Now more than ever, he felt that yearning for her, as he pulled his parka closer around him to keep out the cold.

He blew out the light and settled back in his sleeping back, hopeful that tonight would be the last of the storm, and they could continue to chip away at the remains of an ancient campfire they had discovered earlier that day. What else might it contain of the Neanderthal past?

He fell asleep dreaming of the campfire, and in the flames he saw the faces of his wife and kids smiling their encouragement for him to keep on digging. "We dig what you are doing," their faces seemed to say, as they danced in the flames.

Morning

In the morning, as Darryl peered out of his tent, the snow sparkled in the sun and he was relieved the storm was over. He met his three teammates - Fred, Duke, and Jim -- by a roaring fire where they had started to cook up a breakfast of eggs and coffee. Then, they headed to the cave with the logs and ash. With their shovels, they quickly pushed away the banks of snow in front of the path, and next used their small picks and tweezers to carefully dig through the mounds of ash and dirt around the remains of the ancient campfire.

They dug quietly, carefully, as if they were meditating in a state of reverence for the ancient treasures they might find. It was also a way to imagine what life might have been way back then in order to better consider what they might find.

Suddenly, Darryl's pick struck something hard.

"I think I have something," he yelled out.

All eyes turned to him, and the others watched in silence, as he continue to pick carefully at the dirt, pushing it away into a small pile they would later remove from the cave.

Finally, Darryl saw it, a fragment of bone. As he dug a little more, he saw a dozen other bones. He imagined they were probably placed together in a common burial site, perhaps with some kind of ritual recognizing their death and maybe even praying for their soul to travel to another world for another life somewhere. Or was he just hoping for that outcome, imagining that the Neanderthals might have had the beginnings of faith that drew them together as they buried other Neanderthals in what he now believed must have been a group grave.

Eagerly he kept digging with his pick and tweezer, as his teammates spoke enthusiastically, encouraging him to keep going.

"Way to go!"

"Dig on!"

Once the pit with the bones was exposed, he pulled them out, placing each one, like an honored trophy, in a bag to take back to the lab for further analysis.

"It's a real breakthrough," Fred commented.

"It shows we are on the right track," said Duke.

"Yes," Darryl agreed. "It's like a reward for our months of hard work digging here."

"And it shows we were right," Jim observed. "That's because we choose the location we did based on the rocks and caves suggesting this might be an ideal spot to find Neanderthal remains."

Later that day, after a lunch of dried apricots and beef jerky, they continued digging and bagged more bones and chipped rocks, suggesting the Neanderthals might have created simple tools. Once it grew dark, they toasted their success around a fire by their tents. Though they weren't in a cave, their night of celebration echoed the success the Neanderthals might have had after they brought back game in a hunt.

"Just think what our professors will say," Fred said.

"And the media," said Jim.

"Yes, it'll be great to get some well-deserved glory," Duke agreed. He turned to Darryl. "And you deserve it most of the credit as our team leader and the one who first found the bones."

"But anyone of us could have found them," said Darryl. "We were all digging in the same area together. Anyone of us could have first uncovered the bones."

For a few hours, they went on toasting and celebrating each other for their find. It was just a few small bones, but they shone a light on the life of the Neanderthals many thousands and thousands of years ago.

The Experiment

Back home, after a day of picnicking, walking around a nearby lake, and playing ball in the backyard with Annie and the kids, Darryl headed over to the lab at the university. He carried the bag with the bones, each one preserved in its own inner bag, and he met with Jeremy, the lab director.

"We'd like you to do some age tests, to determine how old these bones are," Darryl said. "Then, we'd like you to arrange for some DNA testing in order to establish that these are, in fact, Neanderthal bones."

"Certainly," Jeremy agreed. "We can sequence each genome and do some comparisons with human DNA to see the segments where the Neanderthal DNA differs."

"Sound good," Darryl agreed.

As he was about to leave, Jeremy stopped him.

"Look, you've been so successful in collecting these bones, I'd like to suggest an experiment we could do with them."

Darryl turned back. "What kind of experiment."

"Well, it could be a real breakthrough, though we'll have to keep it secret at first."

Darryl was intrigued, yet hesitant and suspicious.

"What do you mean a secret breakthrough?"

"This. It's something I've been thinking about since I've read about the new developments with gene editing through the CRISPR gene editing tools and the new procedures of inserting cells from monkeys into mice to make the mice smarter. Other researchers have been using stem cell therapy to cure diseases and prolong life. Some scientists have been successful in cloning several different types of mammals, including dogs and cats. And recently scientists have brought back all sorts of once extinct mammals, such as the Tasmanian tiger, and now there are plans to de-extinct a mammoth."

"Now I'm intrigued. What are you thinking?"

"Here's my idea. You've got all of these bones from Neanderthals. I just need a single bone. I can extract the DNA, insert it into a human stem cell, and then with a human surrogate, we end up with a Neanderthal child with just a very tiny percentage of human DNA left over from the stem cell. What do you think?"

Darryl lapsed into silence. He wasn't sure what to think.

"I don't know. Is it legal to do this? Is it ethical?" he asked finally.

"Look, just about any scientific breakthrough pushes past what's currently known and legal at the time. That's because the breakthrough is so new and innovative. But after it's successful, it gains acceptance and the laws change to accommodate it."

Again, Darryl was silent, thinking.

Jeremy continued. "Just think of all the things we wouldn't have, if scientists and inventors hadn't pushed the barriers of what was then commonly known and accepted. Penicillin. Human flight. You name it. Humans even expanded from Africa to live all over the globe."

Finally, Darryl nodded.

"So if we do this, what are you proposing."

"I just need one bone to extract some DNA. Then, I'll use some stem cells and insert the DNA into the cells to clone it. I'll take care of finding a woman who will be our surrogate. Then, we can raise the child in one of our facilities. And if that works, we can use more DNA from that bone or other bones, so we can create both male and female Neanderthal babies."

"What happens as they grow up?"

"Don't worry. We'll deal with all that when it happens. For now we'll just see if this new technology works. So what do you say?"

Uncertainly, Darryl glanced at the bones he was holding. He thought back to the hard days of digging in Norway. He saw himself playing with Annie and the kids in the backyard. And he imagined the cheering of crowds to celebrate a scientific breakthrough he might create, so he and Jeremy might be like Newton, Galileo, Edison, and other famous scientists who changed the world.

"Okay," he said finally. "I'll do it. So let's begin. I'm still not totally sure about doing this. But I'm willing to take a chance and see what happens."

He handed the bag of bones to Jeremy. Jeremy took it and squeezed Darryl's hand.

"Good. I'll get started and I'm sure everything will be fine."

But would it? Darryl left, still uncertain, yet intrigued, curious to see how things would turn out.

CHAPTER 2: LEARNING IN THE LAB

After a few years, Darryl and his scientist friend Jeremy had a half-dozen Neanderthal children who were three or four years old playing in a small house in Jim's backyard. Three were boys and three were girls, since Darryl and Jeremey felt that would be the best way to compare them as they grew up.

Jeremy brought in some toys they could play with -- a mix of dog throw, squeeze, and chew toys, and some small children's toys -- Lego blocks, soft fluffy Nerf balls, cotton-filled Raggedy Ann and Andy dolls, and some Styrofoam hoops, Frisbees, and swords.

"Now let's see what they do with them," Jeremy said.

For several months they simply observed from the side of the room or through the mirror from an adjacent room. They took careful notes to report each child's progress.

Then, at weekly meetings, they discussed the children's progress.

"They seem to be especially aggressive," noted Darryl at one of these meetings.

"That's right," said Jeremy. "And that goes for the girls as well as the boys. They don't pick up and nurture dolls like other little girls do at a young age. They just throw them around like the boys do. And they play wrestle with them, too."

"Yeah, they're tough little things," Darryl agreed. "So maybe we need to have someone teach them how to be more nurturing."

"Right. They all need someone to help teach and guide them on some basic skills to learn as they grow up."

So Darryl and Jim brought in a nursery school teacher by interviewing several candidates and pledged them to secrecy.

They first brought in Marcy Wilshire, but after she listed her sterling credentials of working at several schools around the country, Marcy began talking about instilling the children early on with a faith in God."

"Every child needs to be taught about God, and they can learn some simple psalms to communicate with Him. Then, if they get in the habit of daily prayer..."

As Marcy droned on, Darryl and Jeremy looked at each other, both knowing she wouldn't work out. When she finished her lecture on how it was very important to guide young children to belief so they would feel loved and at peace with themselves and the world, Jeremy politely told her: "Thank you, Ms. Wilshire. We'll get back to you."

But, of course, they never did.

Then, there was Janice Cotton, and they immediately knew she wouldn't work out either because she was too strict about discipline. After Darryl asked her: "What do you think is the most important thing to instill in a young child?" she responded:

"You've got to show them who's boss from an early age. So I want to make sure the children quickly follow my orders about when to wash, when to go to bed, when to get up, when to do a few small assigned chores. They need to know from the outset what you expect, and if they don't follow your instructions, they need to know there will be consequences."

"What consequences?" asked Jeremy, already knowing he wouldn't let Janice within a few feet of the children.

"Well, they won't get their usual treats the first time they misbehave. Then, they might not get dessert with their next meal. Oh, and I'd tell them why they are being punished each time. After that, they might have to stand in a corner during their playtime. Perhaps they might be spanked a little, too, although I have found that standing in a corner is usually the last thing I need to do. After that they know to behave or else."

"Thank you very much, Ms. Cotton," Darryl said at the end of her diatribe. Then she was gone.

But everything was different when Sarah Loomly arrived, and Darryl and Jeremy knew she was the one, after she answered their question about what she thought was most important for working with young children who don't have parents to raise them.

"You have to show them love," she said. "You have to show them care and compassion. You have to show them you really value them, and you have to guide them in how to behave. For example, you give them examples of what to do."

"What if they don't do what you want?" Jeremy asked.

"Then, you show them how to do it again, and when they do it right you give them an award. It's like training a puppy. You reward them rather than punish them, and if they do something wrong, you distract them so they do something else. Then you show them what you want them to do right, once again."

"Very good," said Jeremy. "I like those answers."

Then Darryl and Jeremy had to make sure Sarah understood the importance of keeping everything confidential.

"You will be teaching some very special children," Jeremy explained. "They look different and act different, and they may be slow to learn and maybe more aggressive than most children. Do you think you can handle that?"

"Oh, yes," Sarah assured them. "I've trained big dogs as well as children, you know."

Finally, it was time to tell Sarah the secret of the program and introduce her to the children.

Darryl pulled a non-disclosure form out of a briefcase.

"We have an NDA for you to fill out," he explained. "You have to keep secret what we are doing here. You can't tell anyone, even your closest friends, husband, or family members."

"Of course," Sarah agreed and quickly signed the form.

"There, I signed it," she said.

After that, Jeremy explained about the children. "They're Neanderthals. They were brought back through the process of cloning ancient cells. Now we want to give them the best life possible today, and we need your help. We want you to train and educate them as best you can. It's the first time anyone has done this, and we can't let anyone know."

"I understand," Sarah said. "And I'll honor your request. No worries."

"Good," said Jeremy.

Then, he led her into the room in the lab where the six children were playing, mostly squeezing their toys, throwing them around, chasing after them, and engaging in play wrestling matches.

Sarah gazed at the playing children for a few minutes, then observed, "Well, I can see I have my work cut out for me. When shall I begin."

"Now," said Jeremy. "And if you need any help from us, just ask. We're ready to help you all we can."

"Good," said Sarah and she went over to greet the children. They looked up, and she said simply, "I'm Sarah," pointing to herself to reinforce her message. Then, gesturing around the room and to herself, she said, "I'll be your teacher."

She hoped by sharing her message in signs as well as words that the children would come to understand what she was saying and maybe learn to speak themselves. She knew it would be difficult, but she thought of how Penny Patterson had taught Koko the gorilla to learn sign language. Maybe she could learn something from that.

She then watched as the children went back to playing, like she wasn't there. She felt that would be the first step -- getting accustomed to her being there. After that, she could start using treats and rewards to help them learn how to understand and speak different things. It would be a process of discovery, and she was ready to guide them along the way.

Darryl and Jeremy watched her from the corner of a room, feeling confident that they had made the right choice of the Neanderthals' teacher.

CHAPTER 3: LEAVING THE LAB

After Sarah had been working with the Neanderthal kids for a year, Darryl and Jeremy felt it was time to move them to a home environment.

"They have to learn to become part of the community," Jeremy said.

"Agreed," said Darryl.

So what did the kids know? How could they function outside of the lab?

Darryl and Jeremy asked Sarah to join them in the office near the playroom where she worked with the kids.

"What's up," she asked.

"We want to find out how well they are doing. We'd like to have the kids raised in a home in the community, and we'd like to see if they are ready," Jeremy said.

"What do you think?" Darryl asked.

"They definitely behave much better," Sarah said. "They have mostly stopped fighting with each other, except maybe over a particular toy that both want. But I have learned how to stop them by separating the fight. Then, I either give them a second toy, or I'll tell one of the fighters he can play with the toy for a few minutes, and then he has to give the toy to the other person to play with. They seem to understand what I am saying and agree."

"That's encouraging," said Jeremy.

"Yes. And they have learned certain words and ideas, such as if I ask a boy or girl to get me a certain flower of a certain color. Or I might ask a child to move something from one place to another, or I can create a race where the kids will try to be the first to do something, like build a small house with logs."

"So they understand some words and simple commands," Darryl observed.

"Yes. That's right," Sarah said. "And I have taught them how to eat with utensils, so they use forks, spoons, and knives, instead of grabbing everything with their hands or slurping things from bowls."

Sarah glanced around the room and pointed to some simple pictures with color splotches on the walls.

"And they can create small works of art, too. They have a sense of pattern and design."

Sarah pointed to three children gathered around a plant. "They have learned to take care of plants, too. I give them water and they water it every day."

Sarah continued on with other examples.

At the end, Darryl stated: "It sounds like you think they're ready."

"Yes, I do. And I think it would be good for them to go to a home. It'll get them out of this isolation in a single room where they only see and interact with each other and me."

So it was decided. The Neanderthal children would soon leave the sanctity of the lab. But where would they go?

Darryl began making calls to local home care facilities and group homes, asking if they could take on six special needs kids. "What kind of special needs?" was the usual question the facility owners or managers asked. Darryl didn't want to say exactly what these kids were like, not yet, until he had picked out a good place and swore the owner or manager to secrecy with an NDA. So he simply compared the children to kids who were slightly retarded with Down Syndrome or Asperger's Syndrome.

A few centers said no, they had all the kids they could successfully handle right now. Some others had run into financial difficulties, since their funders lost interest in their facilities and had invested in something else, so now they were closing and couldn't take on more kids.

But finally they reached Dan Newfounder, who had a facility in the countryside just beyond a small suburban city. He specialized in taking in special needs kids who had been abandoned by their parents because of their difficult to handle disabilities.

"What do you do for them? How do you teach them?" Darryl asked.

"We help them adjust to society," Dan explained. "So we teach them how to socialize with others. And we prepare them to work in simple jobs, such as in rehab workshops, on farms, in factories, and on ranches."

That sounded like the perfect fit, and after Darryl and Jeremy went out to visit the facility with Sarah, they were even more convinced this would be the right place.

"How old are the kids?" Sarah asked, as they walked around the grounds and saw several kids feeding the cows in the barn.

"Anywhere from 2 to 8," Dan said. "Though most are 5 or 6 now. Later, after they get older, we look for a center for older kids who can take care of them. Also, we adopt some to families that want to care for a special needs kids."

After they returned to Dan's office, Jeremy handed Dan the NDA form, and after Dan signed, he explained about the Neanderthal project.

"Of course, it's a big secret," he concluded. "No one can know. Just treat them like regular kids with special needs and tell others the same thing. When the time is right, we'll tell the world, but that's not now."

"Understood," said Dan. "Your secret's safe with me. I only want to do what's best for the kids."

"Good," said Darryl. "We need to avoid any special attention. We don't want the kids to grow up in a fish bowl of media attention and government bureaucracy. That's what would happen if the word gets out now."

"Of course," said Dan. "You have my word. No one will know. Not even the neighbors. And we're pretty isolated out here in the country, which should be ideal."

So it was done. After they got back to the lab, Jeremy started making preparations to transfer the kids, and Sarah agreed to help get the kids ready for the big move.

* * * * * * * * *

The following day, Jeremy led the kids from the lab on a small chartered bus. Darryl sat behind the driver, a burly man who looked like a retired boxer, and he greeted each boy or girl as they got onto the bus.

"Hi...Welcome...We're going to your new home."

Darryl wasn't sure how much the kids understood, but he felt it was important to introduce them to the world of language as soon as possible. Certainly, whatever they learned wouldn't be remotely like what the Neanderthals did in the forests or tundra of Norway so many thousands of years ago. But at least this would be a way to find out how much they could learn and how well they could adjust in their new world.

Meanwhile, as the kids mounted the stairs to the bus and found seats along the sides, they looked around nervously, as if scanning for predators in this strange environment. Then, with Jeremy guiding them, they sat down, one on either side of each row. As the bus started up, they whispered among themselves and looked around some more, even looking up at the top of the bus, as if they expected an animal might be hiding there ready to jump.

"It's okay...Don't be scared...Nothing's going to hurt you," Jeremy sought to reassure them. He wasn't sure if they understood his words, but at least his soothing tone seemed to calm them. Soon they stopped searching around with their eyes and looked forward as the driver stepped on the gas and drove along the driveway leading from the building parking lot into the street.

"We're on our way now....You'll be home soon...We'll be driving through the city."

Jeremy still couldn't be sure if the kids heard or understood him or not, but he was glad to see they were now looking around with eager curiosity as the bus drove on. They tapped each other on the shoulder, grabbed another's arm, and pointed outside the window. The kids' excitement reminded him of his Golden Retriever puppy when he took it in the car for the first time. It hopped up and down in the back seat, as it looked out one window and then the other, seeing everything as new, like opening a gift box for Christmas.

Jeremy sighed with relief, feeling like this was one more sign their experiment was a success, and he glanced over at Darryl, who raised his right hand and curled his thumb and index finger into the "okay" sign.

So far so good, Jeremy and Darryl agreed. Now they just had to get the kids to the group home, where they would spend the next few years, if all went well. And hopefully the media wouldn't find out, so they and the kids could continue the experiment in peace.

CHAPTER 4: THE GROUP HOME

A half-hour later they were at the Happy Hills Group Home, a rambling brown and red ranch house, surrounded by a garden of azaleas and roses and a fortress of oak and eucalyptus trees. The owner and manager, Ernie Masters, met them at the door, ready to show them and the kids around.

As the six kids filed off the bus, he greeted them with a warm welcome.

"Welcome! Welcome! Welcome!" he said enthusiastically to each one, shaking their hands and passing them on to Maggie Waters, his recent grad school assistant, who led many of the workshops and programs.

"Maggie will show you to your rooms, and then we'll show you around."

Soon the kids were settled in, the three boys in one room with three cots, and the three girls in the other. They put down their satchels, which held a change of jeans and a few T-shirts, bounced on their beds a few times, and met Maggie, Ernie, Darryl, and Jeremy in the hallway.

"Now we'll show you around," said Ernie.

As they walked down the hall into the day room, several Down Syndrome boys and girls looked up and came over to greet them. The Neanderthal kids looked at each other quietly, uncertainly, like dogs greeting each other in a dog park.

Then, Ernie broke the ice, turning first to the boys and girls with Down Syndrome.

"Okay, kids. These will be your new neighbors. They're very special kids, just like you're very special. So get to know each other. You'll have plenty of time later, when you all play in the dayroom and at meal times, when you'll all eat together."

All the kids smiled, and Ernie walked on, relieved, as the Neanderthal kids, Maggie, Darryl, and Jeremy followed him. As they walked on, he pointed out the art room, where some children were painting large scenes of mountains and lakes with magic markers and crayons, while a few others were making large blobby clay sculptures on their desks. They passed a gym, with cardio platforms and weights lifting equipment and a big red bouncing ball. He pointed out the rec room with a ping pong table and a large TV screen on one wall. Then, they came to a small classroom with a dozen chairs and a blackboard.

"We want to give the kids an enriched learning environment," Ernie explained. "We know their abilities are limited, but we want to make life seem as normal as possible, so they are better able to adjust to life on the outside."

"Outside?" Darryl asked.

"Why yes," Ernie said. "When they grow up, if they learn to become independent, two or three of them can live together in their own apartment. They can learn to go to the grocery, even go shopping at the mall. The idea is to integrate them into everyday society as much as we can, starting with elementary school age. Then, as they get older, we have a group home for older teens and adults, and we try to help them live as independently as possible "

"That sounds great," Darryl said.

"So we have your trust?" Ernie said.

"You do," Jeremy said.

After that, Darryl and Jeremy left, feeling they had done their part in raising the Neanderthal children to this point. Now it was time for them to become mainly observers, as Ernie and Maggie brought the kids up with other children and taught them as much as they could.

"I feel like a father who just sent his kid to camp for the first time," Jeremy commented on the way back to the lab.

"Yeah," Darryl agreed. "And the more the experiment has been successful, the less they will need us."

Later that day, after the bus pulled in at the lab, Darryl headed home, eager to see his wife and kids, after so many days of quick breakfasts at home and long days at the lab.

"I'll have more time to be at home now," he told his wife Annie, as she put away things from dinner in the kitchen. "Our project just ended."

"What was that?" Annie asked.

"I can't tell you," Darryl said.

Annie looked at him with her eyes half-cocked.

"No, I don't suppose you can," she said, gave a quick scowl, and walked out the back door to the backyard.

He watched her go, uncertain about whether to go after her or what to say. He imagined himself a little like a spy just back from an assignment who has to try fitting into a regular routine again before the next assignment. So no, he couldn't tell her. It would be too easy for her to tell a friend or family member, pledging them to secrecy. Then, they would go tell someone else, in secrecy of course. And so on. So soon the secret would be out, and soon the media would come calling, and that would be the end of an experiment to see if the Neanderthal kids could grow up to live normal lives.

But what could he do to get back in Annie's good graces. Flowers? A nice dinner? He wasn't sure, thinking such gifts would make it seem like he was trying to come back from an ended affair with a mistress. So what?

He went to the window and looked out on Annie puttering around in the garden, while the kids threw balls and jumped on the backyard trampoline.

What could he do? For now he felt very much alone, and he thought of the Neanderthal kids. Maybe they were not part of society yet. But at least they had each other and some other kids they could get to know at the group home, as they tried to learn how to become a part of ordinary life.

At least he had been like a good dad to them for the last few years. Now it was time to move on and see how they were progressing from time to time. If only he could somehow bring Annie and his own kids back into his life the way things had been before. If only he could.

CHAPTER 5: GETTING TO KNOW THE KIDS

Over the next few days, the Neanderthal kids learned their way around the group home, and Ernie began learning their personalities. Joey was the group leader, always eager to explore new things, like the time Ernie found him running down the hall from his bedroom into the dayroom one night.

"No, you can't be here. You have to go to bed now," Ernie told him.

"Why?" asked Joey. "Not sleepy."

Ernie didn't have a really good answer and led him back to his room.

"Sleep is good for you," he explained, as he closed the door.

But early in the morning before breakfast, he found Joey back in the day room walking around and rubbing his hands over the furniture, like he was checking out a new campsite.

"Not sleepy," Joey said again.

Ernie just nodded, and Joey smiled, as if he had won the battle over turf just now.

"Wanted to see things," Joey added, and Ernie just smiled back.

"Sure. Go ahead," he said.

He dubbed Davy the people pleaser. He was always smiling and eager to be around Ernie and Maggie, as they went around doing their tasks for the day, checking on the kids in their rooms or watching them play in the dayroom and backyard. And sometimes as Davy tagged along, he would point and say:

"Me help."

Then, Ernie would find something for him to do, such as take out the lunches and place them on the table before Maggie invited everyone to come eat lunch.

Afterwards, whatever Davy did, Ernie was sure to praise him, patting him on the head and telling him:

"Very good. Good boy."

In turn, Davy raised his head up and down with even a bigger grin, and Ernie thought about how he praised his Golden Retriever Jabs with the same words and pats. Yet Davy seemed to feel real pride when he heard these words, so Ernie guessed it was okay. Kids. Dogs. Just show them you love and appreciate them, and they'll be happy and love you back.

As for Bobby, he was the shy one. He always seemed to hang back and wait to see what others in the group wanted to do. Or if Ernie asked him do something, Bobby looked around for Joey or Davy if they were nearby to see if they were going to do it, too, or agreed that he should do it. For example, one time, when Joey was banging on the piano and Davy was glancing through a picture book with dogs and cats, while Bobby sat on the couch staring off into space, Ernie went over to Bobby and asked him:

"Would you like to go outside and play ball?"

Ernie held up a big red rubber ball.

Bobby looked at the ball and then at Joey at the piano and Davy reading the book. But they didn't look back at him, and he finally nodded.

"Yes, I can play with you."

So Ernie took Bobby outside and began throwing a ball to him.

"Catch it when I throw it," Ernie said.

Ernie stepped back a few feet, and Bobby reached out his hands and tried to catch it. But at first he missed.

"That's okay," Ernie said. "I'll throw it again more slowly."

After a few more tries, Ernie urged Bobby not to be discouraged.

"Keep trying. You'll do it," he said.

After a few more throws, Bobby did catch it, and he jumped up and down excitedly, like he had just gotten a big present. He was like a little dog who had finally found a bone, and Ernie made a note to use the same techniques he did with his dog to help Bobby learn new things. Then, as he did with his Retriever, Ernie took Bobby into the kitchen and brought out a plate with a large chocolate chip cookie.

"It's for you," Ernie said. "Because you have been so good."

At once, Bobby grabbed the cookie, looked up at Ernie with a big grin and puppy dog eyes, and began tearing into the cookie like meat from a hunt.

Then, having thought about the boys, Ernie sized up the girls and noticed that they seemed very similar to the boys in many ways -- Darcy was the leader, Kim the social one, and Suzie the shy one. He also found them much like the boys in being aggressive and ready to fight back if challenged for anything, like who could play with a toy bear or who could make something with the large wooden blocks.

For example, one time he saw Darcy and Judy, one of the Down Syndrome girls, fighting about something. Judy was reaching for a Raggedy Ann doll, when Darcy grabbed it away from her.

"I want it!" Darcy said, as she pulled it away before Judy could grab it.

"No. Me play with it," Judy yelled.

Darcy pulled the doll to her chest like a baby. "No, can't have it. Mine."

Judy began to cry, and Darcy just laughed.

"Loser! Loser!" Darcy said. "So go away. Go cry someplace else. It's mine, all mine."

Darcy smiled broadly as Judy slunk away, like she had just scored a victory.

Meanwhile, Ernie continued watching, not wanting to interfere, and he wondered if Darcy would continue to cradle the doll like a little mother. But instead she grabbed the doll by the arm, twirled it around, and threw it like she was aiming a spear.

"So much for motherhood," Ernie thought, as he walked away and went outside to see what the kids were doing in the backyard.

After he came back inside, he had a chance to observe Kim, the social one, in action. She was sitting with Suzie, the shy one, and two of the Down Syndrome girls, Sheila and Patsy. She noticed the portable radio at one side of the room and brought it over, like she was presenting a deer from a kill and placed it on the small table in front of them. Then, she hit the big power button on top of the radio to turn it on. At once, the pounding beat of a rock band filled the room.

"Now let's dance," Kim said.

A moment later she was on her feet, swaying to the beat and stamping her feet. A few moments later, Sheila and Patsy joined her, while Suzie sat watching the three of them, as if she wasn't sure whether to join in or not.

For several minutes, Kim, Sheila, and Patsy moved back and forth, raising their feet a little higher, stamping them down, and jumping in the air. As Ernie noticed, Kim was always the first to start a new movement, and then the other girls followed along. But Suzie still hesitated, watching the others.

Finally, Kim came over to Suzie, bent over, and motioned for her to follow.

Willingly, Suzie did, and soon she was swaying, stamping her feet, and jumping, too, although she did so with less energy, as if she wanted to follow along to be like everyone else, yet didn't show the wild abandon of the others who seemed truly caught up in the beat of the music. Rather Suzie just mimicked them because they were doing it. But she didn't really feel free herself.

Ernie made a quick note about his observations in a small notebook, so he could remember to report what he observed to Darryl later that night. This way, though Darryl was no longer a day to day participant in the experiment, he could know what was happening. Then, he could better understand what it was like for these Neanderthal kids suddenly brought from many thousands of years ago into a new high-tech age.

CHAPTER 6: A DAY TO REMEMBER

One spring day, when the weather was warm and sunny, Ernie and Maggie took the Neanderthal kids and several Down Syndrome kids, including Judy, Sheila, and Patsy, into the backyard to draw the trees, bushes, and flowers around them. Ernie set out an easel, stool, and colored markers in front of each of them

"Now I'd like you to try drawing what you see around you. You can even draw each other."

Ernie pointed to the paintings and to the different students to make sure the children understood what he said. He picked up a few different colored markers.

"You'll use these markers to draw. Choose any color, and draw what you see."

Most of the kid quickly picked a marker and began drawing, except Suzie who sat staring ahead.

Ernie went over to her.

"What's the matter, Suzie?" Ernie asked.

"Me draw, too?" she asked.

"Yes. Of course," Ernie said. He pointed to her, then back at the board. "You draw, too."

Susie picked up a blue marker and began to draw. It was as if she just needed a personal okay to tell her to go ahead.

Ernie walked around, observing and admiring what the children were doing. Davy was painting two tree trunks, with the large eyes of an animal staring out of it. Bobby was painting a large bush with purple flowers that dotted the plant like Christmas tree lights. Darcy painted a clump of cactuses, and Ernie noticed that the spines looked especially long and dangerous, with pointed tips like spears. As a small butterfly flitted by, Darcy poked at it with her marker. It stopped stunned, and Darcy stabbed again. The butterfly tumbled down and fell on the long tray in front of her. It shook helplessly, flailing its wings, and Darcy eagerly jabbed her marker at it, finally squashing it for good. She smiled broadly, looked around and saw a few other children watching her, and nodded to them, as if acknowledging them for honoring her for her kill. Then, she turned back toward the easel and began to draw a few cactuses with dagger-like hooks.

Ernie moved, and he saw Kim and Suzie engrossed in drawing leaves, stems, and flowers.

"That's nice," he said walking over to each one. "Keep up the good work."

He patted each girl on the shoulder and walked on.

He was curious to see what Joey had drawn. Probably something tough, Ernie thought, as he passed a group of Snap Dragons, who stood like warriors, as they snapped up the flies that flew by.

After he watched a Snap Dragon munch on one of its flies, Ernie headed over to the easel at the end of the row of easels where Joey had started eagerly painting a few bushes with purple huckleberries and a shining sun between them.

But where was Joey? Ernie looked around as he stood in front of Joey's easel.

He went over to Maggie, who was watching the Judy, Kim, and Suzie sketch some flowers.

"Did you see Joey?" he asked.

"No. Why?"

"He's not at his easel."

"Maybe he got tired of panting and went inside to the dayroom or his room," Maggie replied. "Or maybe just a bathroom break."

So Ernie and Maggie went inside looking for Joey.

They looked through the dayroom and checked behind a few couches, in case Joey might be there.

They went into the gym, where a few Down Syndrome boys were lifting small weights or running on the treadmill.

"Did you see Joey?" he asked.

"No...No...No, we didn't," came a series of replies, like a chain of echoes.

Then, Ernie and Maggie headed down the corridor and looked into the room Joey shared with Davy and Bobby. But no. Not there either.

They looked in the bathroom and checked the three stalls.

"He's not in here either," Maggie said, as they headed out of the bathroom.

"Maybe he's back in the backyard drawing," Ernie suggested.

So they went back to Joey's easel and looked all around the backyard.

They stood on the patio looking stumped. Then, feeling frustrated, Ernie went up one row of easels and Maggie went up the other. They stopped besides each of the kids.

"Did you see Joey?" they asked each one, and then: "Did you see Joey go anywhere? Do you think Joey is hiding?"

Each time the kids shook their heads "no" and turned back to their easels, like they didn't want pesky grown-ups interfering with them by asking dumb questions.

But finally, Kim, whose easel was in the row behind Joey's, came over to Ernie and Maggie as they sat at the table with an umbrella on the patio.

"I saw Joey go into the bushes," Kim said. "He said it was a secret. But you looked sad, so I'm telling you."

Ernie and Maggie sat up at attention.

"I hope he won't be mad at me for telling."

"No, no, he won't be," Ernie reassured her.

"But Joey didn't come back. And I didn't want you to be sad," Kim added.

"No, we won't be now," Maggie told her.

As Kim walked back to her easel, Maggie and Ernie went out looking for Joey. They crawled through the bushes and looked around their neighbor's backyard. They drove slowly along the surrounding streets hoping they might see Joey. They stopped at a lot between two houses and walked through it. But nothing. The last thing they wanted to do was call the police and report a missing child, dreading the possibility that the media might follow once the police took the case.

They drove on some more. Then, after they stopped at the homes of a few neighbors, several neighbors drove around helping with the search.

* * * * * * * *

Meanwhile, Joey emerged from the bushes into the backyard of Ernie's neighbor. He noticed a cage with two rabbits near the patio and crept up to it quietly. A dog barked from inside the house, and he grabbed a rake lying by the cage, thinking he might use it if the dog or anyone else came out of the house. But no one was home, so no one emerged from the house, and the dog soon got tired of barking and stopped.

Joey relaxed and gazed back at the rabbits hunched over in their cage.

"You don't like your cage," Joey said to the rabbits, and their ears perked up. "I don't like being in a cage either."

Joey fumbled around for a latch and opened the cage. At once the rabbits hopped out.

"Good. Go little rabbits. Free!"

The rabbits paused and gazed at Joey, their noses twitching. Then, they turned away and began running across the backyard to the bushes.

"Good. Go," Joey said again. "I go, too."

After that, he headed towards the street. Soon Joey was walking past the ranch houses that lined the block, and ahead he saw a bright red sign with six edges. He walked up to it and trailed his fingers around it and over the bright white letters that said "Stop."

After that, Joey stood by the sign watching a few cars go back and forth across the intersection.

He thought it fascinating to see the big cars in different colors -- white, black, gray, and sometimes red -- pass by, and he thought of the great big van that brought him to his home several weeks before. Then, he began counting the number of people in the cars as they passed by -- one, two, and sometimes three.

But where were the cars going so quickly? Why did some suddenly stop, while others kept going? Joey had so many questions, yet he didn't always have the words to ask them, so the fragments of thoughts kept swirling around in his head.

Better to keep on going, he thought to himself. Just see what's out there. Don't let them find you, or they'll take you back to that house with small rooms. Be free and run like the rabbits.

So Joey kept walking.

Eventually, he came to a creek bed by the side of the road and decided to follow it. It wound around like a big blue snake, with the reflections of trees crisscrossing the water as it flowed along.

As he walked along the bank, high above him, he saw the tops of the houses, like the ones he had seen on the street. But now he was down below them, and he felt like he had found a quiet little world. Around him, he noticed a few birds on a nearby bush singing. Then, a striped cat with a furry tail held high stopped across from him and stared. He stared back, as if challenging the cat to show who is boss, and the cat backed off and ran away.

A few minutes later, as he continued watching, an owl climbed out on a tree limb and gazed at him before it flapped away. And after that he saw a brown fawn emerge from the bushes on the other side of the creek. It looked at him curiously, and as he locked eyes with the fawn, it bounded away.

What a wonderful magical place, he thought. It was like a wonderful hiding place where he felt very safe, like the master of this quiet secret world.

But then, he noticed it was starting to get dark, and he felt a chill wind through his T-shirt, as the shadows of the trees began to enclose him.

Better go, he thought to himself, as he felt a twinge of fear ripple through him.

He got up and climbed up the side of hill beside the creek.

Now he was back on the street, and in the distance, he saw the sun hovering low in the sky, surrounded by a yellow-pink glow. Around him the shadows deepened. So maybe it was time to return to the safety of home, he thought. Maybe time to go back into the cage.

But where was he? And how could he get there before it became darker and darker?

Joey turned to head back the way he thought he came. But nothing looked familiar. Confused, he wondered where he was. Maybe in walking around the creek, he had gone further than he thought. Maybe he had come out on a different street. So where was he?

He heard a few cars passing back and forth at an intersection. Maybe that was the way to go. Or was it? At least at a stop sign he had seen the cars coming and going. So that's where he headed now, running faster and faster, hoping to outrun the darkening sky, so he could better find his way.

Soon Joey was at the stop sign. He looked around and saw the ranch houses with large lawns set back along the road. Each way he looked, he saw lines and lines of ranch houses, and in the growing darkness, they looked so similar. Should he turn right or left or go straight ahead to get home? He was unsure what to do, and when an occasional car whizzed by, he felt even more confused by the buzzing, whirring noises. He covered his hands over his ears, trying to shut off the noise that now throbbed in his head like a river passing through pounding rain.

Then, when he looked up, he noticed a strange projection from a tall pole. It looked a little like one of his long and silvery toy rocket ships. As he continued to watch, the strange projection flashed and beeped from time to time. So what was it? It didn't move like a bird with its wings close to its body when it wandered around looking for insects in the grass.

He stepped back to look into the eye of long, silvery projection as it occasionally flashed and beeped.

Suddenly, he heard a loud honking sound that came faster and faster. Moments later, he felt himself being pushed away and down to the street, as he crashed down hard on the concrete. An instant later, he felt a loud rumbling explosion in his head, and when he tried to push himself up, he couldn't move. He fell back exhausted onto the concrete.

At the same time, he heard the loud roar of a car's engine, and moments later, he saw the car that struck him drive off, and he felt a crunching sound and deep stabbing pain, as the car's wheels drove over his leg.

Then,, mercifully, he felt and heard nothing more, as the world around him went dark and pulled him into a deep void.

****

Meanwhile, Ernie and Maggie were growing more and more frantic. As they swept through the neighborhood with a half-dozen neighbors, no Joey, nothing.

As they stood on a corner watching their neighbors, Ernie wondered: "What could have happened?"

"We've got to call the police," Maggie said.

Initially, Ernie hesitated. "I don't know. If we call the police, the media can hear about Joey gone missing on the radio. And then what? The last thing we need is to have a story about these kids out there."

"I know. But this is a kid's life we're talking about. Joey could be in danger. He could be anywhere by now, and we don't know what happened."

Finally, reluctantly, Ernie agreed "Yes, okay."

He pulled out his cell phone. Moments later he was telling the police dispatcher, "There's a missing boy. He ran off about two hours ago, and we can't find him. And now it's getting dark."

"I'll send out a patrol car," she said.

A few minutes later, a police car arrived at the scene, and Ernie and Maggie went over to him.

"We wanted to report a missing boy," Ernie began, and the officer dutifully took notes.

"We'll do what we can," he said.

Then, he called headquarters to report what he had noted, and he sent a file from his laptop to police headquarters.

Ernie and Maggie watched nervously, as the officer moved around his car with his cell phone and reached into his car to send his message. When a few neighbors who came over to find out why there was a police car on the street, they reassured them.

"He's just reporting that Joey's missing," Ernie explained. "The police will help us look."

A few minutes later, as the neighbors dispersed to their homes, since it was now night and hard to search for anything, Ernie and Maggie remained at the corner, as if transfixed, not sure what to do next.

"Maybe he'll come back on his own," Maggie suggested.

"Yeah, maybe," Ernie said. "Where could he go?"

Then, his cell phone rang, and a police officer was on the line.

Ernie's face went white as he listened.

"What's wrong?" Maggie asked.

Ernie put his phone on speaker, so she could hear the message, too.

"I'm sorry to tell you," said the police officer, "but there's been an accident. We took your report of a missing child, and then we got a report of a hit and run a few blocks away. We think it could be your boy. He's at the hospital now. Can you come and identify him?"

"Oh, my God!" Maggie shrieked, as they ran to Ernie's car.

Minutes later, they roared into the hospital parking lot, and then they were at the reception desk, telling the receptionist, "The police just called us to tell us they think our boy is here."

In moments, a nurse was in front of them saying, "Please come right this way."

After that, everything was a maze of corridors and doctors and nurses hurriedly rushing this way and that, until at last they were in the emergency unit.

"Right this way," a hospital orderly told them.

Moments later, they were in the ICU, where a doctor led them over to a boy who lay under a white sheet with tubes and wires running all over his body. But through it all they readily recognized Joey's large pumpkin-like head with heavy brow ridges.

"Yes, that's him," Ernie said, while Maggie began shaking and crying.

"How bad is it?" she sobbed.

"Touch and go," the doctor said. "He's lost a lot of blood, and he has some broken bones. The bones in one leg have been crushed. He's had a concussion and is in an induced coma. But at least he doesn't have a fractured skull."

"At least that's something," Ernie said.

"And what's surprising," the doctor added, "is that his bones are unusually heavy in his skull and through his body. So the effects of the accident aren't as bad as they could be."

"Do you know what happened?" Ernie asked.

"Well, according to the police, a car hit him, knocked him under the car, and ran over his leg. So we're doing what we can," the doctor concluded. "We have surgery scheduled for tomorrow to set the bones and drain any fluids from the inflammation that occurs after any serious injury."

"You'll keep us informed?" Ernie asked.

"Of course," the doctor said.

Then, he rushed off to see another patient in the ICU. Ernie and Maggie walked out of the ICU and down the corridor.

"I guess we can't do anything more here," Ernie said.

"No, we can't. And we should get back to make sure all the other kids are all right. I'm sure the care workers will want to go home for tonight."

"Right," Ernie agreed.

A few minutes later, they were in their car heading home.

"At least we haven't had any calls from the media," Ernie commented.

"No, thank God for that. They probably think this is another routine car accident," Maggie said.

"Let's only hope."

Ernie pulled into the driveway, and they went inside the house, where all the kids were asleep in their beds.

Alonso and Vanessa, the two care workers, greeted them at the door, and smiled happily when Ernie told them, "You can go home now. We're back."

After they left, Ernie and Maggie settled back on the living room couch, relieved to be home. Then, Ernie got up, grabbed a bottle of wine from the cabinet above the sink, and poured a glass of wine for each of them.

"Until tomorrow," he said as he brought the glasses over to the coffee table in front of the couch.

"Yeah, till then," Maggie said, as she picked up her glass. "And all my thoughts and prayers are with Joey."

"My thoughts and prayers, too," said Ernie. "And for the doctors. Here's hoping they can bring Joey back."

They continued to drink their wine in silence, thinking of Joey surrounded by a tangle of tubes and wires and covered by a stark white sheet, as he lay unconscious to the world.

CHAPTER 7: THE AFTERMATH

The next day as Ernie and Maggie headed to their car in the garage, a reporter and cameraman jumped in front of them.

"Are you going to see the boy?" the reporter asked, while the cameraman began filming.

"What's this?" Ernie said angrily.

"Who sent you here?" Maggie asked.

As they spoke, a news van pulled up on the street and then another.

"Are you crazy?" Ernie said, trying to push past the reporter, who stepped ahead of Ernie and blocked his way.

"How darc you?" Ernic scrcamcd at him.

"We can write this story without you. We'd just like a comment from you," the reporter said.

"From me?" Ernie was even angrier.

"What story? Why are you here?" Maggie said, as she saw the reporters and cameramen emerging from the three vans parked on the street.

"Because someone at the hospital told us about the accident and the boy in the ICU."

"But that's confidential," Ernie sputtered.

"Not always," the reporter said. "When there's a big story. we have our sources."

"Big story! What do you mean?" Ernie said.

"Because it's a Neanderthal boy," said the reporter. "Supposedly they died out many thousands of years ago. But now they're back."

"Jesus!" Ernie exclaimed.

He looked around desperately, and Maggie grabbed his hand tightly, as if grabbing a lifeline.

At the same time, the three reporters and three camerapersons from the van were closing in, about to confront him with their notebooks and cameras. Ernie felt like he was about to be encircled and trapped.

"Look, can't you leave us alone?" Maggie begged. "We don't know anything else other than that the boy's in the hospital and fighting for his life."

The reporters scrawled furiously.

"Fighting for his life, you say?" said one of the reporters. He turned to the cameraman beside him. "You got that, didn't you?"

The cameraman nodded, as he continued pointing his camera at Ernie.

"What did they tell you about his injuries?" said the first reporter.

"And what are his chances," the second reporter said.

"Damn you. Damn you all to hell," Ernie screamed at them.

"Please. Please," Maggie begged. "Let us go. Have a heart. We don't know more and have to get to the hospital. Don't any of you have any family members who got hurt?"

Again, the reporters scrawled furiously and the cameras whirred.

"You consider the boy a family member?" the third reporter called out.

Maggie and Ernie ignored him.

"Just let us go," she begged again. "We don't have any more to say now."

This time the reporters and camera people let them through. They separated, half of the reporters and camera people on one side, half on the other, like the parting of the Red Sea. Ernie and Maggie hurried to their car, as the camera people ran after them and filmed, as Ernie opened the garage door with the remote, and he and Maggie quickly got in the car.

As Ernie roared out of the driveway, the reporters and cameramen scurried out of the way and took their last shots of the car barreling down the street. After that, they rushed to their cars and vans to follow Ernie and Maggie to the hospital, hoping to find the answers to their questions there.

* * * * * *

A few minutes later, Ernie and Maggie stood in the corridor with Dr. Matt Perez outside Danny's private room.

"We moved him here," Dr. Perez explained, "since we're not doing anymore procedures. So now it's just 'Wait and see.'"

Dr. Perez led them into the room where Dannie was lying with all kinds of tubes and wires extending from his head and body. They were connected to machines that were blipping out graphs and numbers which showed that Danny was still breathing and getting fluids and nutrition internally.

"What do you think, doctor?" Ernie asked.

"We've seen a little improvement, but we're keeping him in an induced coma for another day or two. And the nurses and doctors are checking him regularly."

Ernie and Maggie watched silently for another minute, until Dr. Perez broke the silence.

"Well, we better go outside now. We'll let you know if anything changes."

"Can you let us know either way?" Maggie asked.

"Yes," Dr. Perez said.

"What about the news media?" Ernie said when they were back in the corridor, the door to Joey's room closed behind them. "How did they know about this?"

Ernie and Maggie glanced down the corridor, relieved to see only doctors, nurses, and orderlies walking about.

"I don't know," Dr. Perez replied. "No one from the hospital staff officially said anything. The media must have learned about this from someone working here who found out and leaked the news. The hospital staff will investigate and try to find out."

"So what do we do?" Maggie asked.

"You don't have to do anything more now. And we'll keep you informed," Dr. Perez assured them.

"Okay. Thank you," Ernie said.

Then, at the door leaving the hospital, Ernie and Maggie were mobbed by a rush of reporters and camera persons, even larger than before. They shielded their eyes from the bright lights of reflectors shining at them.

"How is he?" one reporter shouted out.

"Is he still alive?" said another.

"What do the doctors say?" said a third.

Ernie and Maggie said nothing. They just pushed their way through the crowd, and several reporters moved back to let them through.

Then, like a pack of wolves, the reporters and camera persons chased them to their car in the hospital parking lot.

At last, Ernie and Maggie slammed the doors and Ernie backed up, as a few reporters tapped on the windows and the cameras rolled.

"They're like bees; a swarm of bees," Ernie said to Maggie.

"Just trying to sting," Maggie added.

Then, as Ernie backed into the main lane of the parking lot, the reporters and camera persons spread out to give them room. Ernie stepped on the gas, free at last.

"At least that's over with," Ernie commented, as they drove on the freeway towards home.

"At least until tomorrow," Maggie observed.

But that night, as they watched the news on TV, after the kids in the group home were asleep, they realized it wasn't over at all.

Suddenly, after the national news and a commercial break, the screen showed the reporters and camera persons confronting them at their front door and as they entered and left the hospital.

"And now this breaking story," the news anchor said. "We have just learned that a boy who was hit by a car and is in the hospital fighting for his life is a Neanderthal boy. And that has raised the big questions. 'Are the Neanderthals still alive? And how did he end up in the hospital?' All our thoughts and prayers are with this poor boy to survive. But we have so many questions. So many questions."

Ernie clicked the remote off and slammed it down.

"Crap! Crap! And double crap!" he yelled. "They know! They know!"

"And they'll be here with questions tomorrow," Maggie said, worriedly grabbing Ernie's hand.

"I know. And this is just the beginning of the media nightmare."

"My God! What do we do? And what about all the other Neanderthal kids who are here? I thought we could raise them quietly like the other special needs kids."

"And now we can't. It'll be a media circus," Ernie said.

Ernie staggered up from the couch

"So what can we do?" Maggie said, her voice cracking with anguish.

"I don't know. But I'm going to call our lawyer and tell Darryl and Jeremy what's going on. Maybe they'll know what to do."

Ernie picked up the phone on the table by the couch.

Moments later, his lawyer, Carl Johnson , was on the phone.

"Carl, we have a serious problem," said Ernie. "I need you to tell us what to do."

CHAPTER 8: WHAT'S NEXT?

A few weeks later, Ernie and Maggie were back from the hospital with Joey, who was still very weak and disoriented but on the mend. To get home, they drove through the ever-present throng of journalists who surrounded their car before they could get into the garage, after Ernie opened the door with the remote.

"We heard Joey is home now. How's he doing?" yelled one reporter, sticking a microphone in Ernie's face.

"Will Joey be able to talk to us?" said another, tapping on the window next to Maggie.

"Who's the scientist who brought the Neanderthal's back?" a third reporter called out.

Ernie and Maggie looked straight ahead and tried to ignore them, while Ernie stepped slowly on the gas to move ahead. As he inched forward, several reporters and camera people stepped aside.

Meanwhile, in the back of the car, his leg stretched out in a cast, Joey turned this way and that to see what was going on. He was fascinated to see the people outside of the car holding long handles with bulbs on them, while others dangled big black boxes with long necks from their shoulders. The people seemed so excited and eager, they made him tingle with excitement, too. Maybe they might be fun to play with, Joey thought, like the little metal soldiers he lined up to battle against each other. Suddenly, some of them were shouting loudly and reaching to the car like they wanted something and would fight hard to get it. But inside the car, he felt protected from all that. Then, when he heard the roar of the engine, as Ernie inched forward, he felt very powerful, like these were people to rule over or animals to kill. For now, as he looked down at his outstretched foot in a cast, he couldn't do very much. If only he was strong like the warriors he played with or the soldiers and boxes he saw fighting on TV.

At last, Ernie pulled into the garage and clicked on the remote to shut the garage door. He and Maggie carefully lifted Joey into the fold-up wheelchair they unfolded. They carefully secured him with straps, his leg stretched out ahead of him, and placed a blanket over him to keep him warm. Then, they wheeled him through the side door into the kitchen.

So they were back! Moments later, the two home care assistants and the five other Neanderthal kids rushed forward to welcome them back. The three Down Syndrome kids lingered in the background, a little stunned by all the commotion.

"Welcome back," one of the home care assistants said.

"What can we do to help?" said the other.

"Just take Joey to his room and make him comfortable," Maggie said.

"No bed," Joey said.

"Okay. You can sit up," Ernie told him. "Whatever you're comfortable doing."

"But you need plenty of rest," Maggie said. "You have a lot to heal."

Then, as the home care assistants took Joey to his room, Ernie and Maggie looked through the shuttered blinds to see if the media was still there.

And they were, waiting like jackals in the bush, ready to pounce on their weakened prey.

* * * * * * *

Meanwhile, Joey was delighted to be back in his room with Davy and Bobby. He pulled the blanket to show off his leg in a cast.

"Look," he said. "From the hospital."

He pointed to a few signatures scrawled on his cast.

"The people there wrote these. 'So you remember us,' they said."

Davy grabbed a pen from the small desk by the window.

"Oh, wow! I can write my name, too."

"Write name?" Joey asked.

"Yes. Miss Duncan showed me how."

Moments later, Davy scribbled his name on the cast.

"Me, too," said Bobby, and he added his name.

Then, Joey was curious to look outside. He wheeled over to the window, pushed apart two of the shutters, and peeped out.

"People!" he exclaimed. "Lots of people. With big boxes and long handles. Like around our car."

"Oowee!" said Davy, "I want to see, too."

Then he looked out the window.

Meanwhile, in the backyard, several reporters furiously took notes, while two video and single shot cameras snapped away.

As they did, Ernie and Maggie saw the mad rush of another half-dozen reporters and camera people to the backyard.

"My God!" Ernie called out. "They're going to Joey's room."

Ernie rushed through the house, Maggie just behind him.

As they came into the room, they saw Joey and Davy smiling and waving at the window.

"Oh my God, no!" Maggie shrieked.

Ernie quickly ran over to Joey and pulled him away from the window, while Maggie grabbed and Davy away.

"You can't look out the window!" Ernie said.

"But they smiled and waved at us," Joey said.

"No, no. You don't understand. They can't see you."

"But they saw us! They waved. They friendly."

"And they take our pictures," said Davy.

"Well, you can't do that anymore," Ernie said, realizing that it would be difficult to explain to Joey, Davy, and Bobby or the other Neanderthal children why they couldn't do this.

Ernie reached up and quickly closed the shutters, and he told the home care assistants, who had come into the room, "You have to keep the children away from the windows. You have to keep the shutters closed. You can't let anyone see them."

But now, as much as Ernie and Maggie might want to shut the children away from the world, it was already too late. As they both realized, the reporters already had their notes and the camera people already had their pictures.

"So what can we do?" Maggie asked, as they left the boys' room, leaving the home care assistants behind to calm the boys down.

"I don't know," said Ernie, shutting the door behind them. "That'll be one more thing to ask our lawyer Carl, when he comes over in a little while."

Back in the kitchen, Maggie poured two cups of coffee and handed one to Ernie.

"Let's just chill out for a while. There's not much more we can do while we wait for Carl."

Ernie nodded and they sank down on the living room couch. As they quietly drank their coffee, Ernie clicked on the remote to watch the news. It was almost a relief to see the crisis playing out around the world. It made their own struggle with the media seem that much smaller and less important.

"At least we can be thankful that Joey's getting better," Ernie said to Maggie.

"Yes, thank God he's going to be okay, and the doctor says we can expect a full recovery."

So they settled back, calm now, as they watched jets and bombs flying over Syria, water flooding after hurricanes in Florida, and the President announcing yet another planned military strike in the Middle East.

Then, the local news came on, and this time the anchor led off with photos of Joey and Davy peering and waving through the window.

"Oh, no!" Maggie gasped.

Then, the two news anchors, Rhett Andrews and Sue Winston, began talking about the photos.

"That's quite a story, isn't it," said Rhett. "A local kid got hit by a car and just came back from the hospital."

"So he's going to be okay," said Sue.

"Yes, but that's not the big story," Rhett continued. "It turns out he's a Neanderthal boy, and so is the other boy at the window with him. So that raises the question. How did the kids get here? Are the Neanderthals back, and how?"

"That's right, and we already have some questions from our listeners," Sue noted, raising a handful of sheets of paper from the studio ticker tape. "Here's one. The viewer asks if the Neanderthals are really humans. Or are they more like apes?"

"That's a good one. I don't know."

"And here's another," said Sue, glancing at another piece of paper. "This viewer wants to know: 'What will happen if there's an insurance claim? Will the boy be treated like a child or like a pet who got hurt? And how will the insurance company determine fault? Did the kid just run out in the street so he's at fault? Or did the driver not see him, since it was getting dark, though he should have seen him if he had his lights on?"

"Wow! Now there's a lawyer or lawyer in the making who's wondering about this."

"Or maybe an insurance agent," suggested Sue. "Anyway, this story is sure one that'll get us thinking. And you know this is a story that'll go national. Even international. It'll be a big story everywhere."

"Meanwhile, the authorities are still looking for the driver of the car," Rhett added. "And now a word from our sponsor."

Ernie angrily clicked off the TV.

"God damn it! I can't believe this. We just got Joey back from the hospital, and already people are talking about his legal status and whether he's a real person."

Maggie grabbed his hand to soothe him. "I know. It's terrible what the media can do. But we've got to be strong, at least for Joey's sake and for the other kids."

"I know. I know. But how? What do we say? What do we do?"

Just then, the doorbell rang, sounding like the loud gong announcing the end of a round at a fight.

"At least that should be Carl," Ernie said. "Hopefully, he can tell us what to do."

A few minutes later, Carl, a 40something lawyer specializing in torts and litigation, was sitting across from Ernie and Maggie in the living room.

Ernie quickly explained what had happened, ending with the plaint: "So now the story of Joey and the Neanderthal kids is about to go worldwide, and we're in the middle of this."

"And so are Darryl and Jeremy created these kids in the first place," Carl said. "Plus I imagine the lab where they worked and any surrogate mother or assistants who worked on creating these kids will be involved, too."

"Oh, my, God," said Ernie. "I never thought...We just wanted to help out by giving these kids a good home."

"And so you have. But you have to realize, these are not just like special needs kids with a disability. These kids raise all kinds of questions about what it means to be human and what kind of rights these kids and their creators or guardians have."

"We didn't know," Maggie said weakly.

"I know. But this is likely to be the beginning of a long legal fight, and you better believe me, politicians will get involved. There will be legislators, government officials, and politicians on both sides of the aisle with different points of view. It'll be like the fight over LGBTQ rights and what kind of status and rights they have in society."

"Jesus!" said Ernie.

"And if Darryl and Jeremy were able to create these kids from ancient DNA, that means other scientists might be able to do this, too. So there soon could be more Neanderthal kids elsewhere around the country, around the world. It's likely the scientists and their backers may try to keep all of this quiet at first. But then, almost certainly, the word will get out, because once a scientific or technological breakthrough is successful, others will try to repeat it."

"But legally..." Ernie began.

"Damn the law! To these innovators, the law won't matter, and the law is always playing catch up anyway, when there is a major new technology or scientific breakthrough that changes everything in society."

"You think this will?" Ernie asked.

"Of course I do," Carl said. "So you better be prepared. And I will, too, when the legal suits begin about the accident and about creating and raising these kids in the first place. I'll also be here for you when the media comes calling, and I can speak for you and Joey and the other kids. Or I can help you know what to say."

"Thank you. I don't know what to do next," said Ernie.

"Well, just get prepared. It's going to be a long bumpy ride. It's like being in the Wild West discovering a new frontier. I think the first step is to circle the wagons, and then we'll figure out what we and everyone else involved with these kids needs to do to have a successful ride to get through this mess."

MORE ON THE SERIES

THE NEXT STORIES IN THE SERIES

The following stories have already been set up. They just have to be written. So if you like this first story, let us know, and we'll let you know when the next books in the series are published.

2: Get Smart

3: The New Child

4: The Boxing Match

5: The Accusation

6: The Competition

7: Neanderthal Games

8: The Robbery

9: Rape!

10: Sex Games

11: Strike!

12: Keeping Up with the Neanderthals

13: Between Two Worlds

ABOUT THE AUTHOR

GINI GRAHAM SCOTT, Ph.D., J.D., is a nationally known writer, consultant, speaker, and seminar leader, specializing in business and work relationships, professional and personal development, social trends, popular culture, science, and crime. She has published over 50 books with major publishers. She has worked with dozens of clients on self-help, popular business books, memoirs, and film scripts.

She is the founder of Changemakers Publishing, featuring books on work, business, psychology, self-help, and social trends. The company has published over 150 print and e-books and over 100 audiobooks. She has licensed several dozen books for foreign sales, including the UK, Russia, Korea, Spain, and Japan.

She has received national media exposure for her books, including appearances on *Good Morning America, Oprah,* and *CNN.* She has been the producer and host of a talk show series, *Changemakers,* featuring interviews on social trends.

She brings to *Neanderthal* a special interest in current social trends and new developments in science and technology. Her books in this area include:

The Science of Living Longer: Developments in Life Extension Technology (Praeger) (also turned into a documentary: *The New Age of Aging,* released in June 2019*)*

The Very Next New Thing: (Praeger)

Back to the Middle Ages (AKA: The New Middle Ages - Nortia Press)

Lies and Liars: How and Why Sociopaths Lie (Skyhorse Publishing)

Scammed: Learn from the Biggest Consumer and Money Frauds (Allworth Press).

She also brings her considerable skills as a scriptwriter and executive producer of nine features, documentaries, and TV pilots, which are in distribution, release, or post production through joint ventures with Changemakers Productions. The most recently released include *Driver, The New Age of Aging, Infidelity, Me, My Dog, and I,* and *Reversal.*

She has developed stories in writing memoirs for clients. Among those which have been published are:

At Death's Door with Sebastian Sepulveda (Rowman & Littlefield) (also turned into a TV pilot *Death's Door* and documentary *End of Life*)

From School to War: Growing Up in Hitler's Germany by Wolf Dettbarn (Truman State)

American Justice? with Paul Brakke (TouchPoint Press) (the first of 9 books from American Leadership Books)

She brings to the project an extensive experience in marketing, sales, and promotion, and has turned this hands-on experience into a series of books, including:

Create a Shopify Store to Showcase and Sell Any Products (Changemakers Publishing)

Increase Your Impact and Influence (Changemakers Publishing)

Creating Your First Sales Team (Changemakers Publishing)

Work With Me (Davies-Black Publishing)

Survival Guide for Working with Humans ...Bad Bosses...Employees (AMACOM)

Scott additionally does workshops and writes books about writing and self-publishing to help other writers publish their books. These books include:

How to Find and Work with a Good Ghostwriter

Self-Publishing Secrets

Self-Publishing Your Book in Multiple Formats

Make More Money with Your Book

Conducting a Monthly Social Media Video Campaign

Conducting a Monthly Social Media Campaign on Four Major Platforms

Scott is active in a number of community and business groups, including the Lafayette, Pleasant Hill, and Walnut Creek

Chambers of Commerce. She is a graduate of the prestigious Leadership Contra Costa program and the member of several business networking groups. She does workshops and seminars on the topics of her books and on self-publishing.

She received her Ph.D. from the University of California, Berkeley, and her J.D. from the University of San Francisco Law School. She has received five MAs at Cal State University, East Bay, most recently in Communication.

CHANGEMAKERS PUBLISHING
3527 Mt. Diablo Blvd., #273
Lafayette, CA 94549
changemakers@pacbell.net . (925) 385-0608
www.changemakerspublishingandwriting.com

www.ingramcontent.com/pod-product-compliance
Lightning Source LLC
Chambersburg PA
CBHW070453170726
48291CB00005B/1732